The Name Game

Elizabeth Laird

Olivia Holden

TINY OWL

It's so boring at home.
There's no one to play with...

...and nothing to do.

Then comes a tap
at the window.

Oh! It's a bird!

"Who are you?" I call out.
"Please tell me your name!"

"I'm a magpie, darlin'.

A Jack the lad.
A cheeky chappie.
A jewel thief, if I'm honest.
But a heart of gold
I promise you.

Why don't you give
me a name?

Go on, surprise me!"

"All right then, I will."

This book belongs to

For Iris and Nell – E L
For Daisy Halyna – O H

First published in the UK in 2022
by Tiny Owl Publishing, London

For teacher resources and more information,
visit www.tinyowl.co.uk
#NameGameTO

A catalogue record for this book is available from the British Library.
ISBN 9781910328859

Printed in China

"You're bright black and white, and your feathers sparkle in the sun.

I know what!

You're the Diamond Dodger!"

I know he likes his name because he flaps his wings and cackles before he flies away to perch in a tree.

Oh! Look at the tree!
She's so tall and majestic!
She's just like a queen.

I call out to her, "Please
tell me your name!"

She answers in a growly sort of voice, "Don't be
ridiculous. Trees don't have names. But you
can dream one up for me if you like."

"All right then. I will."

"You look royal and stately, and
your leaves are as green as can be.

I know what!
You're the Emerald Queen!"

She must like her name, in spite of being grand
and grumpy, because she's rattling her leaves
loudly in a friendly sort of way.

A butterfly's landed on the window sill.

I'd better not breathe too hard in case I blow him away.

"Hello, butterfly.
Can you tell me your name?"

He's got a very quiet voice.
I have to bend right down to listen.

I think he says something but I can't be sure.
I'll give him a name anyway.

His wings are as soft as petals and
as red as the heart of a fire.

"I know what!
You're the Ruby King!"

He must have heard me, because he closes
his wings very slowly, twice, then opens
them again before he flutters away.

There's a cat!
Her tail's long and swishy, and her nose is stuck up in the air.

She's pretending not to notice me.

"Hello, cat! Please tell me your name!"

"Since you ask, my humans calls me **Fluffykins**, but that's just wrong for someone as special as me."

"Don't worry! I'll give you a name you'll really like.

You're elegant and proud, and your eyes are as blue as the sky.

I know what!
You're the
Sapphire Princess!"

She's too posh to
admit it, but she likes
her name, I can tell,
because she lifts her
noble paw and gives it
a graceful lick.

I'm still stuck indoors,
but I'm not bored at all.

My new friends are
outside and they love the
names I've given them.

The **Diamond Dodger** sits on the **Emerald Queen**. He's winking his bright black eye, as the **Ruby King** flits past.

"Be careful, Ruby King!" I call out to him.

"Don't let the Sapphire Princess catch you in her paws!"

He flutters away just in time, past
a bee, and a spider, a rose bush,
a puppy and a squirrel.

Oh, and look at that little brown
bird, hopping along the fence!

They all need new names.
I know they do.

"Don't worry, everyone!
I'll give you names that you'll really like."

And I say to myself, what a lovely new game!

Everything, everyone, needs its own name!

A wonderful name!
A beautiful name!
A perfectly gorgeous,
Surprise-me-please name!